T0366036

TWO STONES

story by
RONTEACHWORTH

photography by
TODDWEINSTEIN

TWO STONES

Two Stones, Video Companion:
https://vimeo.com/365127196

"Don't be afraid.
I am here for you to find."

story by
RONTEACHWORTH

photography by
TODDWEINSTEIN

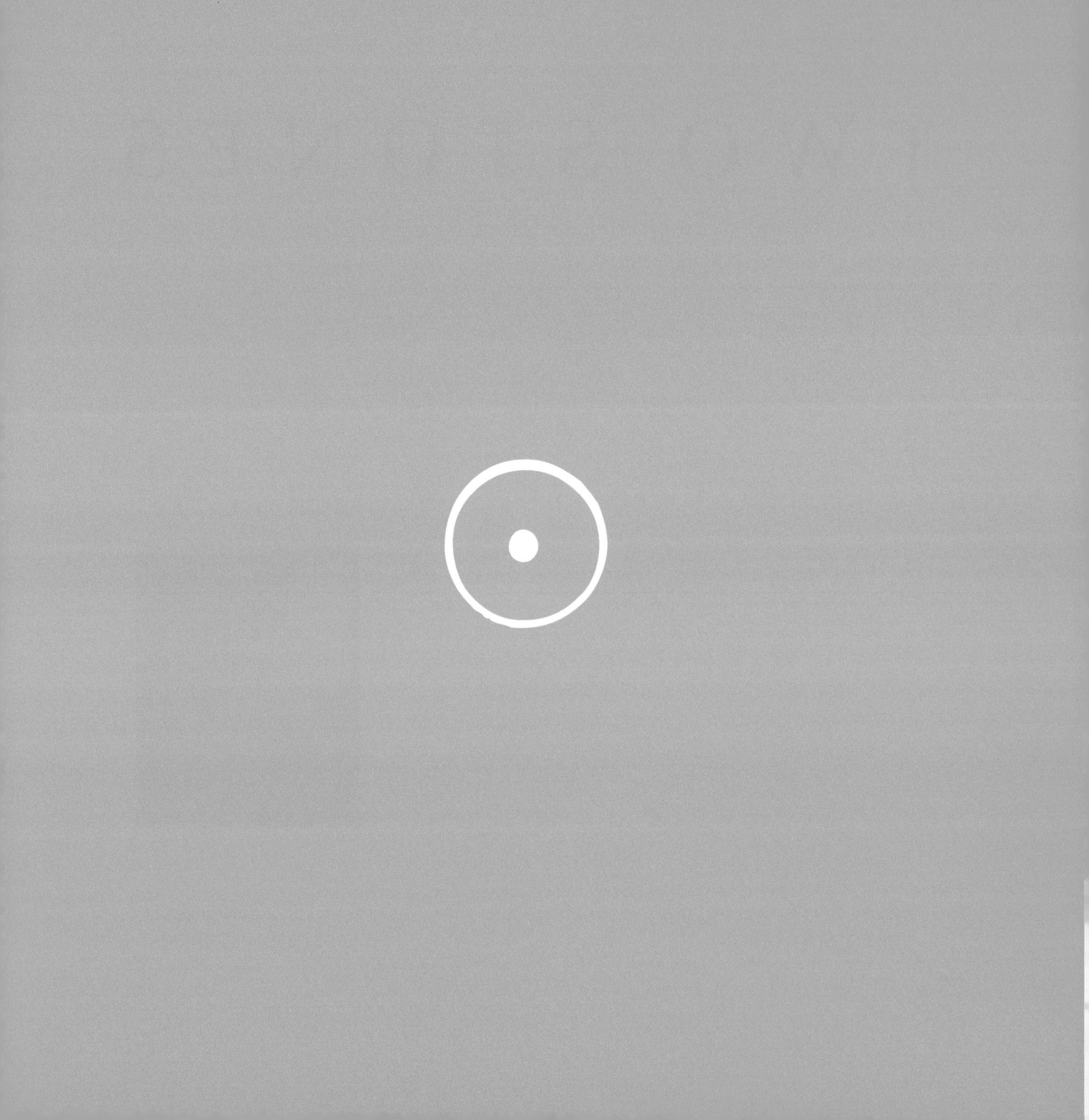

Eventually, everyone goes on a summer vacation with their parents. After weeks of anticipating the end of school, summer finally appears and the trip begins.

Her parents were arguing and she felt like crying. Analisa curled up in the back seat of the car, placed the headphones on her ears and turned up the volume. The long ride up north to the white clapboard cottage with the screened-in porch had really taken its toll, and the family unloaded the over stuffed station wagon in total silence.

Analisa left the small cottage and walked far through the windblown sand dunes to the beach. The late afternoon sun was working its way down ward along the secluded stretch of beach on the large great lake. Pools of sunlight streamed through breaks in the clouds and danced on the surface of these gently formed swells of water.

Analisa's long flowing hair was barely moving in the afternoon breeze as she stood still along the shore. She was preoccupied with the thoughts of her parents' argument. She remembered how they had parted after disagreeing so much during the long drive, and she was worried.

Maybe they'll never talk to each other again, she thought.
Maybe they'll get divorced.

A bit young to be alone, she began walking along the water's edge with one eye open and one eye closed. On the horizon the silhouette of a small fishing boat shimmered in the still summer air. Analisa heard only the sounds of the lake water coming ashore and the distant seagulls searching for their dinner in the dark blue water of the bay.

Placing one foot directly in front of the other, she made light impressions in the wet sand and watched her footprints disappear at the water's edge.

I wish these feelings would disappear, she thought.

As Analisa walked along, the water ran over feet and between her toes. She noticed hundreds of small round stones that lay everywhere, sparkling like jewels in the sun, polished shiny by the water that washed over their surface in an endless rhythm of movement.

She stopped and used her one hand to shade the brightness of the setting sun. It was getting late and she now felt nervous about being alone on the beach.

Suddenly she heard a quiet voice "Hello."

Startled, Analisa took a step back and looked around in all directions, but she saw no one.

"I must be hearing things", she said to herself.

"Hello," the voice repeated. The sound seemed to be coming from the water itself.

No longer startled but now somewhat frightened, Analisa stared hard at the beach where the voice seemed to have originated. All she could see was a smooth and perfectly round stone that glistened in the sunlight.

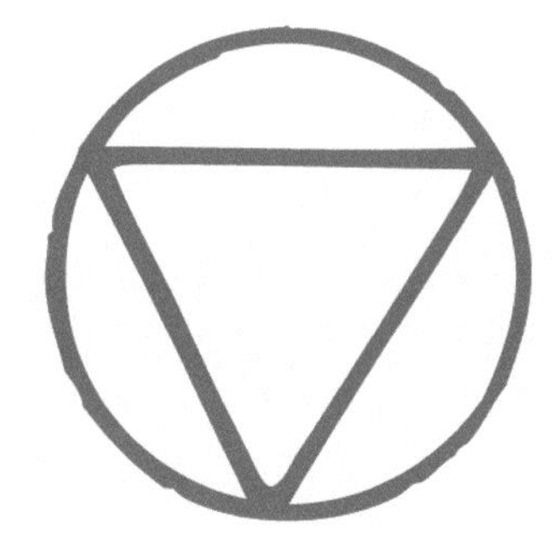

"Hello," the voice repeated. It was the stone!

"Don't be afraid. I am here for you to find. I have been waiting a long time. Please don't be afraid."

"Stones don't talk!" Ana said aloud, amazed.

Then she watched carefully as the stone moved and turned itself ever so slightly.

"Please don't leave me," said the stone." I need your help. Please, will you help me?"

Still thinking, *It moved all by itself?*
She whispered hesitantly: "What can I do?"

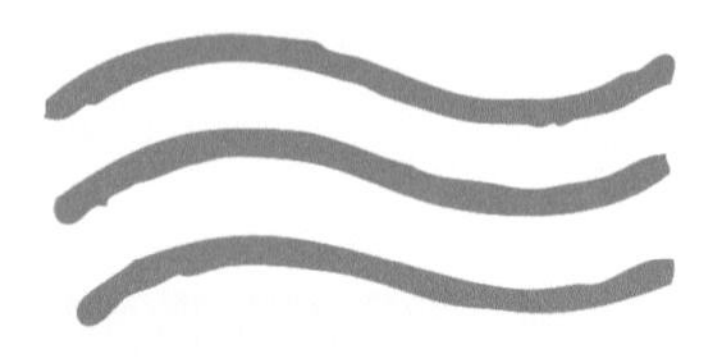

"Just pick me up," the stone replied, "Walk south along the beach, and I will tell you when to set me down. Oh please! It would mean so much to me . . . and for you as well."

"Me?" asked Ana. "What will happen to me?"

A sudden breeze came up, and she could no longer hear the gulls on the bay. The fishing boat had disappeared. Analisa saw no one else on the beach. Though she was still afraid, the stone's voice was kind and gentle. She decid-ed to follow her intuition. *After all,* she thought, *what harm is there in picking up a stone?*

She reached down and picked up the stone up from the beach, and began to walk slowly without saying a word.

Just moments later, she saw the sun reflect from a second stone.
Its shape was the same, but darker. Like the one she now carried in her hand, the second stone glistened brightly and stood out from all the rest.

"Set me down next to that one," the stone said from inside her hand.

Analisa walked slowly to the new stone and, without hesitation, gently placed the stone in her hand next to the one lying on the beach so that the two were just barely touching.

The incoming waves washed over her feet several times as she stood looking at the two stones in amazement. No more words were spoken. She heard the sound of low flying seagulls once again, and she looked over her shoulder into the slow setting sun for a moment to watch the graceful birds hover in the breeze, almost still.

Though it was only for a few seconds since she looked away, when Analisa looked back at the two stones, she saw that they had begun to dissolve and slowly disappear.

At that very same moment, she noticed a man and a woman gradually begin to appear in the distance. She realized they were walking toward her at the same time the two stones had disappeared. The man and the woman approached her, holding hands.

"Ana, where have you been?" her mother called. "We've been looking everywhere for you! You've walked too far down the beach by yourself."

"We were getting worried about you," her father said gently. "Are you all right?" Analisa ran and leaped at her mother, her face falling deep into her mother's dress. She hugged her ever so tight, while trembling ever so slightly inside.

“I don’t know what happened,” Analisa said softly as her father knelt down into the sand.

“It’s getting late, Analisa. We’ve got to get back to the cottage before it gets much darker. We’re just glad you’re all right.”

As they turned to start back through the hills of beach sand, Analisa was clinging to her mother, when her father asked, “Do you collect beach stones? ”

He extended his hand and opened it to offer his daughter two stones.

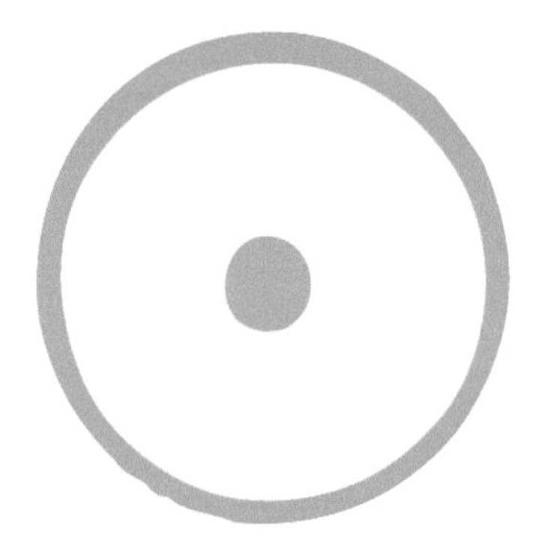

“I picked these up just for you.
We love you, Analisa, ...we would
never want anything to happen to you.”

Analisa took the stones from her father's hand without speaking and held them tightly. She was happy to be with her parents. They walked back through the dunes in the fading light to the clapboard cottage with the screened-in porch. She held the two stones for hours, wondering whether they were the stones that had disappeared and would they speak again.

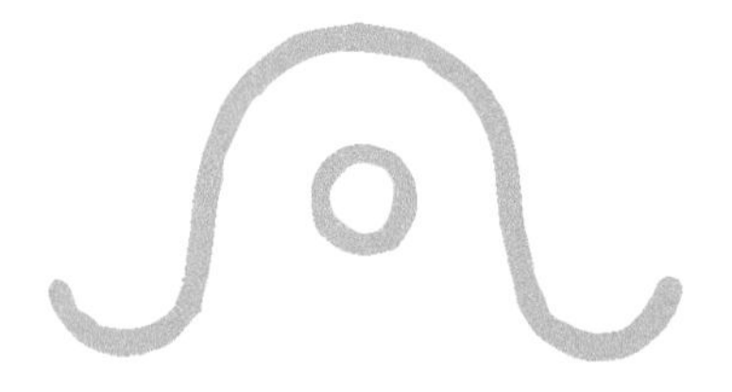

But neither stone ever spoke, and over time Analisa came to question what had happened on the beach that late afternoon. The two stones at the beach had brought everyone closer together. The rest of their vacation was wonderful and flew by without a single argument.

As she grew older Analisa often thought about the events that after noon at the beach. But no matter what...

...She always made a point to keep the two stones that her father had given her, next to one another on her bedroom dresser, just barely touching.

UNIVERSAL SYMBOLS

These symbols are a personal collection cross-referenced from multiple sources over a period of years. They are universal symbols represented in many cultures from around the world.

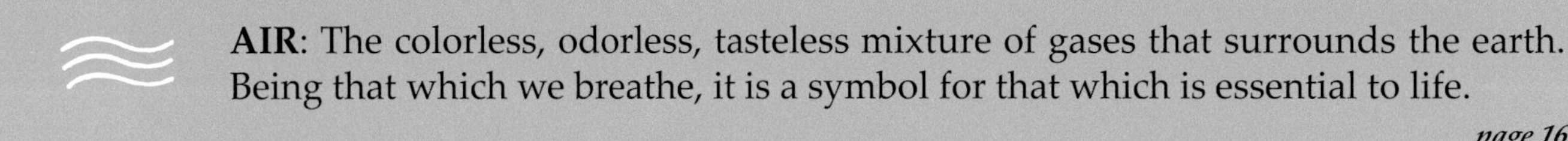

AIR: The colorless, odorless, tasteless mixture of gases that surrounds the earth. Being that which we breathe, it is a symbol for that which is essential to life.

page 16

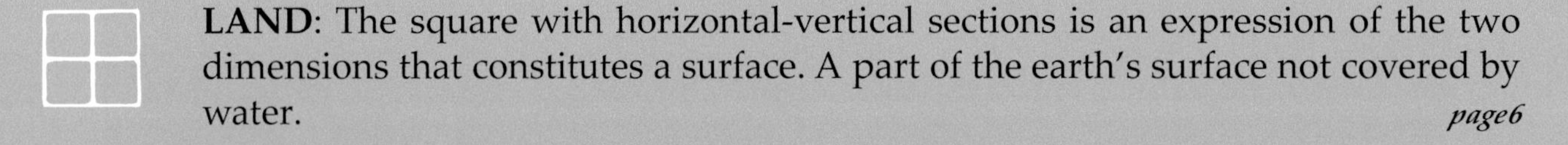

LAND: The square with horizontal-vertical sections is an expression of the two dimensions that constitutes a surface. A part of the earth's surface not covered by water.

page6

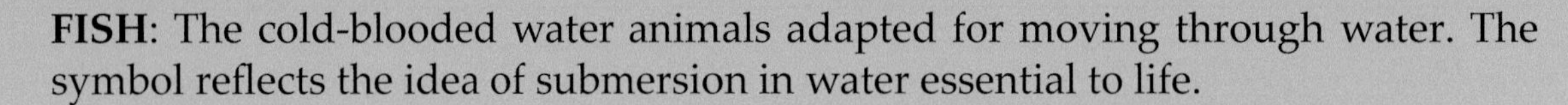

FISH: The cold-blooded water animals adapted for moving through water. The symbol reflects the idea of submersion in water essential to life.

page 8

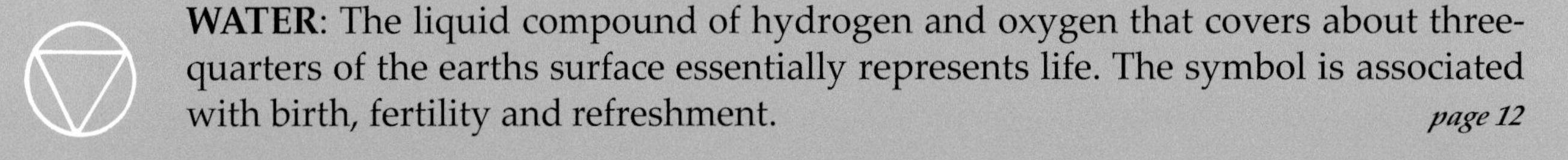

WATER: The liquid compound of hydrogen and oxygen that covers about three-quarters of the earths surface essentially represents life. The symbol is associated with birth, fertility and refreshment.

page 12

MEASUREMENT: The size, amount, capacity or degree of something determined by a comparison to standard. The symbol from the Egyptians describes methods used as a standard of comparison determining measurable results.

page 16

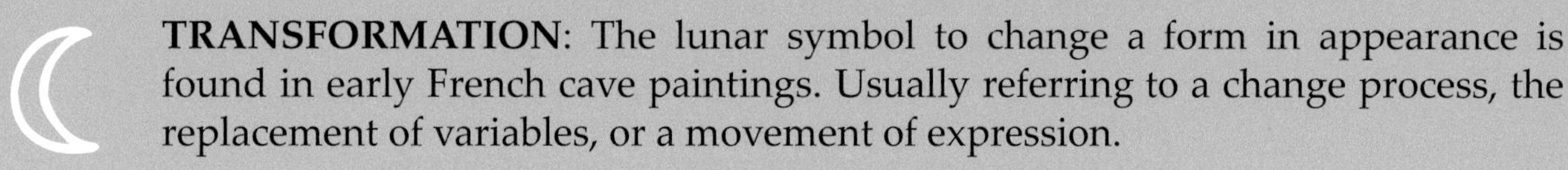

TRANSFORMATION: The lunar symbol to change a form in appearance is found in early French cave paintings. Usually referring to a change process, the replacement of variables, or a movement of expression.

page 20

UNIVERSE: One of the oldest ideograms found on Neolithic caves, the circle often represents the sun or moon and the dot symbolizes the center. Together they represent all matter and space that exists, considered as a whole.

page 24

ALCHEMY: The medieval system of beliefs and practices where there is a transformation of metals. The symbol has been used to describe a process where man is in search of himself and the meaning of life.

page 26

ENERGY: The ability to act or put forth effort with the mind or body. The early symbol depicts an expansion of movement using the design of a spiral.

page 26

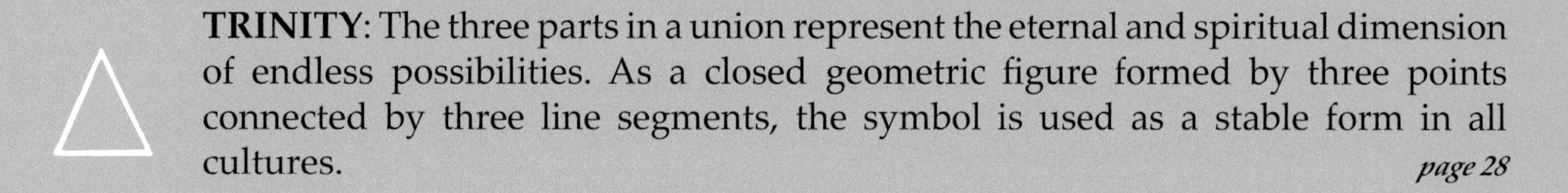

TRINITY: The three parts in a union represent the eternal and spiritual dimension of endless possibilities. As a closed geometric figure formed by three points connected by three line segments, the symbol is used as a stable form in all cultures.

page 28

Copyright © 2009 by Ron Teachworth. 546777

All rights reserved. No part of this book may
be reproduced or transmitted in any form or by
any means, electronic or mechanical, including
photocopying, recording, or by any information storage
and retrieval system, without permission in writing from
the copyright owner.

This is a work of fiction. Names, characters,
places and incidents either are the product of the
author's imagination or are used fictitiously, and any
resemblance to any actual persons, living or dead,
events, or locales is entirely coincidental.

To order additional copies of this book, contact:
Xlibris
1-888-795-4274
www.Xlibris.com
Orders@Xlibris.com

ISBN: Softcover 978-1-4363-6174-3
Hardcover 978-1-4363-6175-0
EBook 978-1-9845-8252-2

Library of Congress Control Number: 2008907053

Print information available on the last page

Rev. date: 06/05/2020

http://www.ronteachworthliterary.com

Printed in the United States
By Bookmasters